Holly's New Friend

Martyn Hobbs

HELBLING LANGUAGES

www.helblinglanguages.com

Holly's New Friend
by Martyn Hobbs

First published 2011

ISBN 978-3-85272-334-1

Series editor Maria Cleary
Activities by Martyn Hobbs
Illustrated by Lorenzo Sabbatini
Design and layout by Pixarte
Printed by Athesia

About this Book

For the Student

Listen to the story and do some activities on your Audio CD

Talk about the story

beat• When you see the blue dot you can check the word in the glossary on pages 62-64

For the Teacher

Go to our Readers Resource site for information on using readers and downloadable Resource Sheets, photocopiable Worksheets, Answer Keys and Tapescripts. Plus the full version of the story on MP3.

www.helblingreaders.com

For lots of great ideas on using Graded Readers consult Reading Matters, the Teacher's Guide to using Helbling Readers.

Level 1 Structures

Present simple of *be*	*A / an*
Have got	*The*
There is / there are	Subject pronouns
Present Simple	Object pronouns
Can (ability and permission)	Plural nouns
Present continuous	Countable and uncountable nouns
	Some / any
Like / love / hate / don't like doing	
Imperatives	Adjectives
Short answers	Possessive adjectives
Who? What? Where? What colour?	Possessive *'s*
How much? How many?	Demonstrative adjectives and pronouns
Adverbs of frequency	*very*

Contents

Before Reading	6
Holly's New Friend	11
After Reading	54
Glossary	63

Before Reading

1 Look at the picture and answer the questions on pages 8 and 9.

The Animal Rescue Centre

Before Reading

1 **Label Holly's bedroom on pages 6 and 7 with the words below.**

a) poster b) magazines c) CD
d) lead e) petition

2 **Label the animal rescue centre on page 7 with the words below.**

a) kennel b) cage c) basket
d) bowl e) tail f) paws

3 **The things in the pictures on pages 6 and 7 are important to the story. Why are they important? Can you guess? In groups write a scenario. Include all the things from exercises 1 and 2 in your scenario. Remember to look carefully at the pictures! Then tell the class. Choose the best scenario.**

4 **Talk about the pictures on pages 6 and 7.**

- What are the people doing?
- What type of films does Holly like?
- What type of films do you like?
- Have you got a pet? What is it?
- What's your favourite animal? Why?

5 Listen and match the names with the pictures.

David Grace Zadie Mum Dad Sophie

a) ....

b) ....

c) ....

d) ....

e) ....

f) ....

6 Work in groups. Is it a good idea to have a pet dog? What are the good things about it? What are the bad things?

A PET DOG

Good things

a good friend

Bad things

can be smelly

The front door opens and closes with a bang. Holly throws her school bag onto the floor and calls out, 'I'm home!'

No answer.

So she tries again.

'Hello! I'm home!'

No answer.

The house is silent. It sounds empty•, but she knows it isn't. Her dad is working in his office upstairs. Her mum is working in *her* office in the loft•. And her sister is in her room, listening to music or sending text messages to a new boyfriend. Sophie always has a new boyfriend! So Holly takes off her school jacket, drops it on her bag, and walks into the kitchen.

She gets a glass of orange juice from the fridge, goes into the conservatory• and sits down in her favourite chair. It's an old deckchair•. Her mum doesn't like it in the conservatory. She and Holly have arguments about it, but Holly always wins.

The garden is very still in the dark afternoon. Most of it is neat and tidy• with boring short grass, boring straight flowerbeds and boring straight paths. Only Holly's Nature Garden (that's her name for it – her mum calls it The Jungle) looks wild and exciting. It contains big dead sunflowers, bushes with lots of berries•, tall grasses and old vegetables with strange shapes.

Then Holly looks at her plants and herbs• in the conservatory, safe from the winter weather. There's basil, rosemary, sage and loads• of other plants. They grow tall and wild and fill up her side of the conservatory with their lovely perfume.

But the conservatory is divided just like the garden. On the other side her mum keeps all her boring flowers in tidy pots with labels on them. There isn't a leaf or bit of dirt on the floor. It's neat and shiny like a supermarket.

Holly sits and looks out at the empty garden. She listens to a single bird singing in the darkness. And then she starts thinking unhappy thoughts.

'I'm just like that sad lonely• bird. Nobody is interested in me. My parents only think about their work and my sister only likes boys and shopping. I don't know why I live in this house!'

But she knows that today is special. Today things are changing. She can't wait any longer. It's time to talk to her parents.

Two months earlier...

Christmas is over. Holly's dad is working in his office. Her mum is shopping at the sales. Sophie is hanging out• with her friends. Holly is lying on the sofa and watching the Movie Channel. First, she watches an old Lassie film. It's in black and white and really boring, but Lassie is a beautiful dog and he always saves people in trouble. Then she watches a Tintin cartoon. Holly isn't very interested in Tintin, but she likes Snowy, his pet dog. Finally she watches *The Wizard of Oz*. There's a girl in the film with a dog called Toto. Toto is Holly's favourite dog and she always feels a bit sad when the film ends.
Holly switches off the TV with the remote•.
The house is silent.

One month earlier...

Holly is reading a magazine. And she isn't very happy.

Pets are for life

Puppies are so cute. And kittens are so sweet. People think they make really great gifts at Christmas. But a few weeks later, they get bored with their new pets. They don't want to take their dogs for a walk. Cats can scratch the furniture. And every pet takes up a lot of their time.

Dogs want to play, they want attention, they make noise.

They're expensive, too. Not just for food, but think of all those vet's bills!

So what happens? Every year, people put their pets in their cars, drive for kilometres, then leave these poor animals at the side of the road.

They abandon them!

13

Holly puts down the magazine. Her eyes are red.

One week earlier...

Holly is carrying a big bag of bird seed from the pet shop. She has a bird table in her Nature Garden – and the birds eat the food really quickly! But while she's walking home, she hears a sound – a dog is barking somewhere. There's nothing strange about that, but this dog sounds upset. Holly listens carefully. She's right. This dog is in trouble. She runs towards the sound and stops at the entrance to an alleyway•. A dog is standing at the far end. But two boys are there, too. They are holding sticks and waving them at the dog.

Holly doesn't think twice.
'Stop that!' she shouts.
The boys turn around, surprised.
'Leave that dog alone•!' Holly says. She speaks loudly – but she can hear the fear in her voice.
'What do you want, little girl?' the tall one asks.
'Are you looking for trouble•?' the short one asks.
As they start walking towards her, the dog runs past them and along the road.
'Hey!' the tall one says. 'That's your fault, little girl. I want to talk to you.'
He waves his stick at Holly.
But Holly doesn't want to talk to him. She throws the bag of bird seed at them, then quickly runs away.

One hour earlier...

It's only four o'clock, but it's cold and grey and getting dark. Holly and Zadie are on their way home from school, talking about their day – about all the good things and the not so good things.
When they get to Zadie's house, her mum opens the door – and a big funny brown dog jumps out of the house and into Zadie's arms. He nearly knocks her over•!
'Hey Scamp! Take it easy!' says Zadie, laughing. But Scamp just licks• her face and wags his tail•.

'Do you want to come in?' asks Zadie's mum.
Holly nods• and smiles.
But half an hour later, she is walking home again, alone.
And she's thinking about another boring evening.

It's time for Holly to talk to her parents.
So she gets up from her deckchair and climbs• all the way• to the loft. The door is open so Holly goes straight into her mum's office. She is doing something on the computer.
'Are you busy, Mum?'
'What was that, darling?'
Her mother doesn't look up.
'I want to talk.'
'Oh, just a minute,' says her mother. She clicks on the keyboard, takes off her glasses and turns to look at her daughter.
'What is it, Holly?'
Holly coughs, takes a deep breath, then starts to explain.
One minute later her mother says, 'No, Holly. That's impossible.'
And Holly turns around and walks out of the room.

Holly walks noisily downstairs to her father's office. She knocks on his door, waits for him to say, 'Come in!' Then enters. Her father's on the phone. He's *always* on the phone, and when he isn't on the phone he's working on his computer. She waits and rehearses• in her mind what she plans to say. Finally he presses a button on his mobile and looks at her.

'Dad, can we talk?'

'Sure. But not for long. I have to make another call. What is it?'

'I've got an idea,' says Holly.

Thirty seconds later...

'Absolutely not!' says her father.

So Holly walks out of the office (leaving the door open), goes into her own room and slams• her door shut.

The door opens. It's Sophie.
4
What's up, Holly? You sound really mad.
This is so unfair!
What is it?
Pets at Christmas
I'm really upset about all the dogs and cats at Christmas.
What do you mean?
People get bored with their new pets and then they abandon them. It's really sick.
I agree. I feel really sorry for those animals.
Well, Mum and Dad don't understand at all.
What can we do about it?
Pets at Christmas
Animal World

I want to get a pet from one of the rescue centres. I want a dog.
You want a dog?
Uh huh.
A dirty, noisy, smelly dog?
Not all dogs are dirty and noisy...
Animal W
Yes, they are! I agree with Mum and Dad. I don't want a horrible dog in this house.
Sophie quickly leaves the room...
and a book hits the door one second later!
Animal World
Pets at Christmas

The next day at school, Holly is quiet. Very quiet.
She spends the whole time looking out of the window during the science lesson.
'What's up with Holly?' whispers• Grace.
'I don't know,' says Zadie. 'She's acting really weird•.'
Jack decides to have some fun. He takes a sheet of paper from his notebook, folds it, and makes a paper plane. He aims carefully, then throws it at Holly. It flies through the air and lands on her desk – but Holly doesn't even notice. Unfortunately, Ms Jones the science teacher does.
'What do you think you're doing, Jack?' she asks loudly.
'It's a scientific experiment,' says Jack.
Everybody laughs... except Holly and Ms Jones.
Holly is still looking out of the window, thinking.

At lunchtime, Holly eats her sandwiches then walks on her own round the playing field.
'Is Holly OK?' asks Ricky.
'I'm not sure,' says David. 'She seems really worried about something.'
But during their maths lesson, Holly suddenly says:
'That's it!•'
Everybody looks at her.
'What is 'it'?' asks Ms Cooke, the maths teacher.
'Oh, erm, nothing, Ms Cooke. Sorry.'
But when Ms Cooke looks away, Holly smiles.
After the lesson, her friends all want to ask Holly the same questions.
'Are you all right? What are you thinking about? What's going on?'
'I have a plan, guys•,' says Holly. 'And I need your help.'

On Saturday morning, Holly's parents are in the kitchen having coffee.
'Where's Holly?' asks her dad, Alan.
'She's in her room,' says her mum. 'I think she's doing her homework.'
'Well, I'm glad that silly business• about the dog is over,' says Alan.
And they smile.
In fact, Holly is chatting online with David. They are writing a song together about a dog. It doesn't take them very long.

On Sunday morning, Holly meets Ricky and Zadie at Grace's house. The girls are in a band and Ricky (he's brilliant at computers and all the things Holly doesn't understand) records her new song.

On Monday morning, Holly starts her campaign•.

Stage One•

Holly's alarm goes off at 6:00 am. She immediately gets up, turns on the light, and gets her CD player. She goes outside her parents' bedroom and puts the CD player on the carpet. She puts in a new CD, turns the volume to maximum, and presses 'Play'. Then she quickly runs back to her room and jumps into bed.

A terrible noise fills the house.

I WANT A DOG!
I WANT A DOG!
IT'S ONLY FAIR!
I WANT A DOG!!!!

Suddenly the bedroom door opens. Two shocked white• faces stare• at the CD player. Holly's parents cover their ears in horror.

Stage Two

After school, Holly goes back to Ricky's house. Ten minutes later, she continues her journey home. She is carrying a big bag full of paper.

Before she goes to sleep, Holly sets her alarm clock for 3:00 am. When the alarm goes off, Holly gets up and goes into action.

Holly's parents go downstairs in the morning and they can't believe their eyes. On every wall and door, on every window and mirror, on the fridge, on the table, on the ceiling and on the floor, there are posters. There are even posters on their computer screens!

Stage Three

In the evening, Holly presents her parents with a long sheet of paper.
'What's this?' her father asks nervously.
'It's a petition.'
'A petition?' repeats her mother.
'That's right. It's a petition for me to have a pet dog. Look, these are the signatures• of nearly everyone at my school.'
Holly's parents look at the long list of names. Luckily, they don't read all of them. Lots of the names are in Holly and her friends' handwriting! Then her parents look at each other and Holly's mother nods.
'All right, Holly,' says her father. 'We know this is important to you. You can have a dog.'
Holly gives a loud happy shout.
'But,' adds her mother, 'it's *your* responsibility. Do you understand?'
'Of course,' says Holly with a big smile.
'Now where do we get a dog?' asks her father.
'From an animal rescue centre!' says Holly.

On Saturday morning...
Well, here we are.
Willow Farm
Animal Rescue Centre
Oh, wow! Look! Those are goats!

Harry Clarke, the owner, shows them around the rescue centre.
We don't only look after cats and dogs. We have rabbits and guinea pigs...
I can't believe there are so many animals here.
... ducks and geese...
... and ponies and donkeys, too!

Harry takes them to the kennels.
We have twenty dogs here at the moment. It's always bad after Christmas.
We can't take all of them, Holly.
They're all so sweet!
Oh look at him!
He looks a bit strange to me.
Why don't you choose a beautiful dog?
He's so cute. I love him.
Are you sure?
Definitely! He's my dog!

And so Holly gets her pet dog. She's so happy – and the dog is happy, too! Now there's an important decision to make. The dog needs a name!

'Why don't you call him Brownie?' her mother says.

'Brownie? Why?' asks Holly.

'Because he's brown,' she explains.

'That's silly,' says Sophie. 'What about Jack Sparrow?'

'Like in *The Pirates of the Caribbean*?' asks Holly.

'That's right. He looks like a pirate with an eye patch!'

'I prefer a traditional name like Rex or Rover,' her father says.

'Oh no, Dad, that's awful!' says Holly. 'I want to call him Eco.'

'What?' they all ask.

'Eco. Like ecological.'

'You're joking,' says Sophie.

'No, I'm not,' says Holly. 'That's his name. Come here. Eco!'

And Eco wags his tail.

That night, Holly puts her glass of water next to her bed, reads for ten minutes, then falls asleep. And she finds herself in a beautiful forest. The trees are tall above her head and they are covered in big, green leaves. Small birds fly between the trees, singing all the time. And as Holly walks through the forest, she sees smiling green frogs and red and purple butterflies. There are no people anywhere. There are no houses or cars or computers. And there are no car radios with their booming• sound systems. There is only the sound of the moving leaves and birdsong and insects and... something else.

In her dream, Holly stops and listens.

Lap, lap, lap.

What is that noise? It sounds like water. Is it rain? But Holly can see the sky and it is clear and blue. Is it a river? Or a stream•?

Lap, lap, lap.

Holly walks towards the sound.

Lap, lap, lap.

The sound is quite loud now. It seems very close.

Lap, lap, lap.

Holly wakes up and rubs• her eyes. She isn't dreaming. But she can still hear the sound.

Lap, lap, lap.

Holly turns on the bedside lamp and sees Eco. He is drinking from her glass of water! He wags his tail, jumps onto the bed and licks her face.

Before school, Holly takes Eco for his first morning walk. She feels very tired. It's really cold and dark – and it is so early!
But Eco doesn't mind. He pulls on the lead, stops, sniffs•, pulls again, sees a black cat, tries to chase it and nearly pulls Holly off her feet•! He sees a huge dog and tries to play with it (the big dog is quite frightening). And then he chooses a tree. Eco stops, sniffs at the tree trunk, looks up, sniffs again, and makes a decision. This is the perfect place!
Holly looks away and waits.
When Eco is finished, she takes a plastic bag from her pocket and picks up the dog mess•.
Yuck!

Holly gets back from the walk and realises it's late. She quickly eats a slice of toast, grabs her bag and jacket, and runs out of the front door. 'Close the door, Holly!' shouts her mother. But it's too late.
When Holly gets to school, everybody is sitting quietly in the classroom. They are doing a french test. Holly says sorry to Mr Maxwell and sits down next to Zadie. Then she looks at the test. The questions are really difficult!

Holly is trying to write a conversation in French when she hears Jack laughing.
'What's so funny, Jack?' asks Mr Maxwell.
'That, sir!'
Jack is pointing at the window. The rest of the class look at the window and they all start laughing, too.
A dog is looking into the classroom.
Eco!

It's dark when Holly takes Eco for his evening walk. Holly runs along the road with him, but it's difficult because Eco often stops to investigate interesting bushes and trees. And he often tries to catch birds or play with twigs• and fallen leaves.
After about ten minutes, it's Holly's turn to stop suddenly. She sees two boys on the corner. They are standing under a streetlamp•. One of them is tall, the other one is short. They are the boys from the alley! Holly feels nervous•. She decides to take a different route. She doesn't want to go near them with Eco.

A few days go by. Then...

It's raining outside. But where's Eco?
8
Eco! Come in!
Eco enters... and the trouble starts.
Oh look at your dirty paws! Come here!
Stop that dog at once!
GLAM
Eco!
CRASH!!!

Eco runs upstairs!
Oh no.
My favourite vase!
Where is he now?
Is he in your dad's office?
Get out of here!
No! He's in Sophie's room!
You horrible dog!
Don't panic, Sophie.
Stay cool.
That's my new sweater!
Do something, Holly!
Come on, Eco.
Let go. Please!

That evening...

'That dog is your responsibility, Holly,' says her father. 'And it is out of control•.'

'But he's only a puppy.'

'He's a horrible little dog. Look at my sweater!' says Sophie.

'It's a horrible sweater anyway,' Holly replies.

'Holly!' says Sandra.

'All right, I'm sorry, Sophie,' says Holly.

Sophie still looks very angry.

'That dog needs rules,' her father continues.

'But Eco's a free spirit!' says Holly.

'No, he isn't, Holly,' says her father.

'Eco is a pet in our house.'

'He needs to know the rules. And the first rule is, keep him in the kitchen at night. Put his basket in the corner. And keep the kitchen door shut. I don't want Eco in the rest of the house. Do you understand?'
Holly doesn't answer.
'Holly, do you understand?'
'Yes.'
'Good.'

But that night, Holly lies awake in bed.
She waits and waits.
When she thinks everybody is sleeping, she gets up and pulls on her socks. Then she creeps• downstairs.
One of the steps on the staircase makes a creaking noise•.
It's an awful noise.
Holly stops.
But nobody wakes up!
So Holly carries on and goes into the kitchen.
Eco is awake. He wags his tail and Holly gives him a hug•.
'Poor little Eco. It isn't fair. You don't want to sleep in this rotten• old kitchen.'
She picks him up and carries him into the conservatory.
'You can sleep in here,' she says.
'There are lots of lovely plants.'
Then Holly puts his basket near her herbs.
She goes back into the kitchen, closes the kitchen door, and silently goes back to her room.

Holly wakes up early. Her parents mustn't find Eco in the conservatory! So she goes downstairs and enters the kitchen. There are leaves and dirt on the kitchen floor.
'Oh no,' says Holly. 'Eco? Where are you?'
There's no answer.
So Holly enters the conservatory and it's a disaster.
First she sees her mum's plants and flowers. They aren't all neat and tidy now. The plants are lying on their sides or on the floor. And the pots are broken into a hundred pieces.
Then Holly looks at her side of the conservatory. It is a scene of total chaos. And Eco is sitting in the dirt and leaves.

'All my herbs! All my beautiful plants!'
Eco wags his tail.
'You bad dog!' Holly says. 'Come here!'
Eco looks confused. He doesn't move.
Holly opens the door to the garden.
'Get out. Do you hear me? I have to clean up this mess before Mum and Dad get up.'
Eco still doesn't move.
Holly gets really angry now.
'GET OUT YOU STUPID DOG!' she shouts angrily.
This time Eco runs into the garden.
But Holly doesn't have time to clean up the conservatory. She hears voices behind her.
'Oh Alan, look at this!'
'What's going on, Holly? Where's Eco?'
Holly looks at her parents, then she looks at the garden.
Eco isn't there.

Holly looks in the garden...
Eco! Where are you?
Next she checks in the road...
Eco!
After that she searches the house...
It's hopeless, Mum.
It's time for school now.
But don't worry.
He'll come back.
But when she gets home... he isn't there.
Eco! Eco!
So Holly calls her friends...
Hi Grace. I'm so worried.
I really need your help...

They all search for Eco.
Even Sophie helps.
We're all looking for Holly's horrible dog. It's sooo cold!
Holly sometimes thinks she sees him... but she's wrong.
Oh, no!
Finally, they meet outside the house.
I'm sorry, Holly. We can't find him tonight.
We can try again tomorrow.

Before she goes to bed, Holly leaves a bowl of dog food and a bowl of water outside the conservatory door.
Then she goes to bed and lies there in the dark, listening and listening.

She wakes up suddenly in the early morning. She jumps out of bed and rushes• downstairs. She opens the conservatory door.
The food bowl is empty. But the water in the other bowl is frozen•.
'Eco!' she calls out.
She waits.
'Eco!' she tries again.
But the garden is empty and still•.
A window opens upstairs.
'Don't stand outside in the cold, Holly,' her father says. 'It's freezing.'
Holly looks up but everything looks strange and blurred•.
She's crying.

Ricky is waiting for her outside the school gate.
'Is there any sign of Eco?' he asks.
Holly sadly shakes her head.
'We can find him, Holly. Look at this.'
Ricky takes a big sheet of paper from his bag. It isn't a petition this time. It's a poster.
'Oh, Ricky, that's really kind of you.'
Holly feels like crying again.
'Hey, Holly, it's no big deal. I love making things on my computer.'
Then Holly looks at the poster again.
'A £100 reward•? I haven't got that money,' she says.
'Don't worry, Holly. We can all help.'

Holly's friends stick up the posters all over town.
But nobody phones her with news of Eco.
She leaves food and water in the garden every night.
Every morning there's no food and no Eco.
And every night, Holly sits by her window, looking down into the garden.
Sometimes she hears a noise and thinks it's him.
Sometimes she thinks she can see a shape in the darkness.
But she knows there are cats out there, and foxes, too. Maybe they are eating Eco's food.
She remembers the dog with the funny face at the animal rescue centre. She thinks of his silly eye patch. She thinks of his wagging tail.
And she remembers that last morning...

A full moon is shining above the houses and the trees. It travels slowly across the sky. It never stops moving.
It has no home to go to.
Holly thinks of Eco out there in the cold night, all alone and scared.
She remembers those two horrible boys.
And she looks, and she listens, and she can't sleep.
Tears• drip• from her eyes.
A grey blanket of cloud creeps across the sky, eating up all the stars.
It moves across the face of the moon, too. And now even the moon is invisible.
And in the light from a streetlamp, Holly sees white flakes falling from the sky. They fall silently past her window to the garden below.
It is snowing.

When Holly looks out of the window in the morning, the world is white. The roofs of the houses are white, the trees are white, the grass is white. But she sees something else, too.
She pulls on her clothes and trainers, runs downstairs, and opens the conservatory door. The bright snow dazzles her eyes• and the cold air makes her cheeks turn red. But there, in the snow, she clearly sees little shapes going from the food bowl to the end of the garden. These aren't human foot prints. They are paw prints! Holly follows them across the garden, crunching• the snow under her feet.

They go under a gap in the fence beneath the old tree to the garage. The garage door isn't completely closed. The paw prints stop at the entrance. An animal is in there. A fox? A cat? Or even...
'Oh please, please,' she says softly.
Holly pushes up the door and steps inside.
It's very quiet in the garage. Her parents' car is in the middle, and along the walls are shelves filled with all the old things that don't fit in the house. Her dad's tools•, Holly's old toys, boxes, bags – all the things they don't want but don't want to throw away.
In the corner, under a pile of cardboard boxes, and lying on an old blanket, she sees a dark shape.
It opens an eye.
It opens another eye.
Its tail starts to wag.

Eco!

Before Holly goes to school, there's a meeting in the kitchen. Her mother, father, sister and dog are all there. The conclusion is:
Holly can keep Eco,
BUT
she must take him to a dog training school.
Holly doesn't like the idea, but she hasn't got a choice. And secretly, she knows it is the only solution.
So Eco learns to sit when Holly says, 'Sit!'.
He learns to come when Holly says, 'Come here!'.
He goes to his basket when...
You get the idea!
And the amazing thing is, Eco really enjoys it. For him, it's one big game. And he doesn't get into trouble!

Holly is walking through a beautiful forest.
The sun is shining through the tall trees and the thick, green leaves.
Birds are singing on the branches and butterflies are dancing in the air.
Then she hears a noise.
It's a splashing, lapping sort of noise.
Water!
Holly runs towards the sound and finds...
Eco in the middle of a stream! He is playing, jumping around and chasing a stick.
But this isn't a dream. Holly doesn't wake up and find Eco licking her face or drinking from her glass of water.
She smiles.
'Come here, Eco!' she calls out.
Eco looks up and sees Holly.
And then he runs to her.

After Reading

Understanding the story

1 **What happens in the story? Read and number the sentences in the correct order.**

a) ☐ Eco makes a big mess – and runs away!
b) ☐ One morning Holly's parents have a terrible surprise.
c) ☐ Holly finds Eco in the garage.
d) ☐ Holly asks her father for a pet dog.
e) ☐ Eco goes to a dog training school.
f) ☐ Holly's family visit an animal rescue centre.

2 **Match the sentences in Exercise 1 with the pictures**

3 **Why are the following characters important in the story? Discuss your ideas with a partner.**

Sophie

David

Ricky

Alan

Grace

4 **Read the sentences and then choose the correct word or words for each space.**

a) Holly wants a pet dog because she feels ....
1 happy 2 worried 3 sad

b) Holly sees two boys being horrible to a ....
1 cat 2 dog 3 bird

c) Holly and her friends record a new ....
1 petition 2 song 3 campaign

d) Eco breaks Sandra's favourite ....
1 vase 2 mirror 3 glass

e) Holly sees Eco's paw prints in the ....
1 grass 2 dirt 3 snow

5 **Holly really wants a pet dog. What do you really want? Talk about it with your partner.**

After Reading

Vocabulary

1 Circle the adjectives in the word snake.

silenttidyhugeboringexpensiveemptyconfusednervous

2 Complete the speech bubbles with the adjectives from exercise 1.

a) I feel so .... I've got three exams tomorrow!

b) There's nothing on TV tonight. All the programmes are ....

c) I want to buy a new skateboard but it's very ....

d) The house is .... I can't hear a thing!

e) There's nothing to eat in the fridge. It's .... !

f) My room isn't .... In fact, it's a mess!

g) I don't know what to do. I'm really ....

h) My uncle lives in a .... house. It's got ten bedrooms!

3 Match the verbs with the pictures. Then write sentences to say what is happening in each picture.

a) search b) point c) throw d) dream

4 When can you use these phrases? Match.

a) ☐ Take it easy.
b) ☐ You're joking.
c) ☐ This is so unfair!
d) ☐ I'm not sure.
e) ☐ What's up?

1 You don't know something for certain.
2 You think someone is worried or sad.
3 You want someone to relax.
4 You don't believe someone.
5 You think something is wrong.

5 Complete the conversations with the phrases above.

a) **Mum:** You have to tidy your room.
Lisa: ……………………………………………

b) **Tom:** I'm really angry now!
Nick: ……………………………………………

c) **Liam:** What's the answer to number 5?
Sarah: ……………………………………………

d) **Jake:** ……………………………………………
Poppy: I can't find my mobile.

e) **Joe:** My brother is a famous actor.
Toby: ……………………………………………

After Reading
Grammar

Practise the Present Continuous

1 Look at the picture and answer the questions.

a) What is Zadie doing?

....

b) What is Holly wearing?

....

c) Where is Zadie's mother standing?

....

d) What is Scamp doing?

....

e) What is Holly thinking?

....

2 What do you think these people are doing at the moment? Write sentences.

a) My mother ....

b) My teacher ....

c) My best friend ....

Practise the Present Simple

3 Complete the sentences with the correct form of the verbs in the box.

give	work	think	sit	like	look

a) Holly often .... in her deckchair and .... at the garden.
b) Her parents .... at home.
c) Her sister Sophie .... dogs.
d) Holly's friends .... her lots of help.
e) Holly .... Eco is the best dog in the world!

Practise asking questions

4 Do an interview with Holly. Complete the questions with the words below.

who	where	what	how

You: ....'s your dog's name?
Holly: His name's Eco.
You: .... old is he?
Holly: He's about a year old.
You: .... colour is he?
Holly: He's brown.
You: .... is he at the moment?
Holly: He's in my room.
You: .... is he doing?
Holly: He's sleeping on my bed!
You: .... takes him for a walk?
Holly: I do!
You: .... often do you take him for a walk?
Holly: Twice a day. Sometimes three times a day.

After Reading

Test

1 Listen and tick (✓) the correct picture.

a) 1 ☐

2 ☐

3 ☐

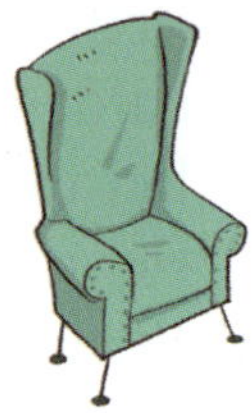

b) 1 ☐

2 ☐

3 ☐

c) 1 ☐

2 ☐

3 ☐

d) 1 ☐

2 ☐

3 ☐

Glossary

11 **empty:** there isn't anybody or anything inside it
loft: a room just under the roof of a house
12 **berries:** all types of fruit that grow on bushes, such as blackberries and raspberries
conservatory: a room with glass walls and roof to keep plants from cold weather
deckchair: 
neat and tidy: carefully arranged and in order
13 **herbs:** plants used in cooking for their pleasant smell and flavour
loads: lots
14 **lonely:** unhappy because it has no friends
15 **hanging out:** spending time with
remote (remote control): gadget to operate a television from a distance
17 **scratch:** make marks with their claws
vet: animal doctor
18 **alleyway:** a narrow street, a dark passage
19 **leave that dog alone:** stop hurting that dog
looking for trouble: wanting to cause an argument
20 **knocks her over:** makes her fall down
licks: touches with his tongue
wags his tail: moves his tail from side to side
21 **nods:** moves her head up and down meaning "yes"
22 **climbs:** goes up
way: distance
23 **rehearses:** prepares and practises
slams: shuts making a loud noise
24 **mad:** very angry
sick: cruel
25 **rescue centres:** where animals are saved from danger and abandonment
26 **guys:** people; friends
That's it!: I've found the solution!
weird: in a strange way
whispers: says in a low voice

28 **business:** matter under discussion
campaign: plan of action
29 **stage one:** the first phase or action of Holly's campaign
stare: look in a fixed way
white: pale
31 **signatures:** names that people write on a document
33 **cute:** pretty and attractive
35 **booming:** very loud
36 **rubs:** moves her hand over
stream: small river
37 **dog mess:** dog's excrement
off her feet: making her lose her balance
sniffs: uses his nose to find a smell
39 **nervous:** anxious; frightened
streetlamp: tall post in the street with a lamp
twigs: small branches fallen off trees or bushes
41 **let go:** don't hold
stay cool: keep calm
42 **out of control:** impossible to manage
43 **creaking noise:** small sound of wooden floor when you walk on it
creeps: moves very slowly and quietly
gives him a hug: puts her arms around him
rotten: horrible
48 **blurred:** out of focus; not clear
frozen: transformed into ice
rushes: goes very fast
still: quiet; silent
49 **reward:** (here) money for finding something
51 **drip:** fall
tears: liquid from the eyes when you cry
52 **crunching:** crushing with a lot of noise
dazzles her eyes: blinds her with too much light
53 **tools:** things you use to do a job